ENUMA ELISH: THE EPIC OF CREATION

Translated by L.W. King

ENUMA ELISH: THE EPIC OF CREATION

Table of Contents

ENUMA ELISH: THE EPIC OF CREATION..1
    Translated by L.W. King..1
    THE FIRST TABLET...2
    THE SECOND TABLET..6
    THE THIRD TABLET..10
    THE FOURTH TABLET..14
    THE FIFTH TABLET...19
    THE SIXTH TABLET..21
    THE SEVENTH TABLET..22

ENUMA ELISH: THE EPIC OF CREATION

Translated by L.W. King

Kessinger Publishing reprints thousands of hard-to-find books!

Visit us at http://www.kessinger.net

- THE FIRST TABLET
- THE SECOND TABLET
- THE THIRD TABLET
- THE FOURTH TABLET
- THE FIFTH TABLET
- THE SIXTH TABLET
- THE SEVENTH TABLET

ENUMA ELISH: THE EPIC OF CREATION
THE FIRST TABLET

When in the height heaven was not named,
And the earth beneath did not yet bear a name,
And the primeval Apsu, who begat them,
And chaos, Tiamut, the mother of them both
Their waters were mingled together,
And no field was formed, no marsh was to be seen;
When of the gods none had been called into being,
And none bore a name, and no destinies were ordained;
Then were created the gods in the midst of heaven,
Lahmu and Lahamu were called into being...
Ages increased,...
Then Ansar and Kisar were created, and over them....
Long were the days, then there came forth.....
Anu, their son,...
Ansar and Anu...
And the god Anu...
Nudimmud, whom his fathers, his begetters.....
Abounding in all wisdom,...'
He was exceeding strong...
He had no rival –
Thus were established and were... the great gods.
But Tiamat and Apsu were still in confusion...
They were troubled and...
In disorder...
Apru was not diminished in might...
And Tiamat roared...
She smote, and their deeds...
Their way was evil...
Then Apsu, the begetter of the great gods,
Cried unto Mummu, his minister, and said unto him:
"O Mummu, thou minister that rejoicest my spirit,
Come, unto Tiamut let us go!

ENUMA ELISH: THE EPIC OF CREATION

So they went and before Tiamat they lay down,
They consulted on a plan with regard to the gods, their sons.
Apsu opened his mouth and spake,
And unto Tiamut, the glistening one, he addressed the word:
...their way...
By day I can not rest, by night I can not lie down in peace.
But I will destroy their way, I will...
Let there be lamentation, and let us lie down again in peace."
When Tiamat heard these words,
She raged and cried aloud...
She... grievously...,
She uttered a curse, and unto Apsu she spake:
"What then shall we do?
Let their way be made difficult, and let us lie down again in peace."
Mummu answered, and gave counsel unto Apsu,
...and hostile to the gods was the counsel Mummu gave:
Come, their way is strong, but thou shalt destroy it;
Then by day shalt thou have rest, by night shalt thou lie down in peace."
Apsu harkened unto him and his countenance grew bright,
Since he (Mummu) planned evil against the gods his sons.
... he was afraid...,
His knees became weak; they gave way beneath him,
Because of the evil which their first-born had planned.
... their... they altered.
... they...,
Lamentation they sat in sorrow
....
Then Ea, who knoweth all that is, went up and he beheld their muttering.

[about 30 illegible lines]

... he spake:
... thy... he hath conquered and
... he weepeth and sitteth in tribulation.
... of fear,
... we shall not lie down in peace.

ENUMA ELISH: THE EPIC OF CREATION

... Apsu is laid waste,
... and Mummu, who were taken captive, in...
... thou didst...
... let us lie down in peace.
... they will smite....
... let us lie down in peace.
... thou shalt take vengeance for them,
... unto the tempest shalt thou...!"
And Tiamat harkened unto the word of the bright god, and said:
... shalt thou entrust! let us wage war!"
... the gods in the midst of...
... for the gods did she create.
They banded themselves together and at the side of Tiamat they advanced;
They were furious; they devised mischief without resting night and day.
They prepared for battle, fuming and raging;
They joined their forces and made war,
Ummu-Hubur [Tiamat] who formed all things,
Made in addition weapons invincible; she spawned monster-serpents,
Sharp of tooth, and merciless of fang;
With poison, instead of blood, she filled their bodies.
Fierce monster-vipers she clothed with terror,
With splendor she decked them, she made them of lofty stature.
Whoever beheld them, terror overcame him,
Their bodies reared up and none could withstand their attack.
She set up vipers and dragons, and the monster Lahamu,
And hurricanes, and raging hounds, and scorpion-men,
And mighty tempests, and fish-men, and rams;
They bore cruel weapons, without fear of the fight.
Her commands were mighty, none could resist them;
After this fashion, huge of stature, she made eleven [kinds of] monsters.
Among the gods who were her sons, inasmuch as he had given her support,
She exalted Kingu; in their midst she raised him to power.
To march before the forces, to lead the host,
To give the battle-signal, to advance to the attack,
To direct the battle, to control the fight,
Unto him she entrusted; in costly raiment she made him sit, saying:

ENUMA ELISH: THE EPIC OF CREATION

I have uttered thy spell, in the assembly of the gods I have raised thee to power.
The dominion over all the gods have I entrusted unto him.
Be thou exalted, thou my chosen spouse,
May they magnify thy name over all of them the Anunnaki."
She gave him the Tablets of Destiny, on his breast she laid them, saying:
Thy command shall not be without avail, and the word of thy mouth shall be established."
Now Kingu, thus exalted, having received the power of Anu,
Decreed the fate among the gods his sons, saying:
"Let the opening of your mouth quench the Fire-god;
Whoso is exalted in the battle, let him display his might!"

ENUMA ELISH: THE EPIC OF CREATION
THE SECOND TABLET

Tiamat made weighty her handiwork,
Evil she wrought against the gods her children.
To avenge Apsu, Tiamat planned evil,
But how she had collected her forces, the god unto Ea divulged.
Ea harkened to this thing, and
He was grievously afflicted and he sat in sorrow.
The days went by, and his anger was appeased,
And to the place of Ansar his father he took his way.
He went and, standing before Ansar, the father who begat him,
All that Tiamat had plotted he repeated unto him,
Saying, "Tiamat our mother hath conceived a hatred for us,
With all her force she rageth, full of wrath.
All the gods have turned to her,
With those, whom ye created, they go at her side.
They are banded together and at the side of Tiamat they advance;
They are furious, they devise mischief without resting night and day.
They prepare for battle, fuming and raging;
They have joined their forces and are making war.
Ummu-Hubur, who formed all things,
Hath made in addition weapons invincible; she hath spawned monster-serpents,
Sharp of tooth, and merciless of fang.
With poison, instead of blood, she hath filled their bodies.
Fierce monster-vipers she hath clothed with terror,
With splendor she hath decked them; she hath made them of lofty stature.
Whoever beholdeth them is overcome by terror,
Their bodies rear up and none can withstand their attack.
She hath set up vipers, and dragons, and the monster Lahamu,
And hurricanes and raging hounds, and scorpion-men,
And mighty tempests, and fish-men and rams;
They bear cruel weapons, without fear of the fight.
Her commands are mighty; none can resist them;
After this fashion, huge of stature, hath she made eleven monsters.

ENUMA ELISH: THE EPIC OF CREATION

Among the gods who are her sons, inasmuch as he hath given her support,
She hath exalted Kingu; in their midst she hath raised him to power.
To march before the forces, to lead the host,
To give the battle-signal, to advance to the attack.
To direct the battle, to control the fight,
Unto him hath she entrusted; in costly raiment she hath made him sit, saying:.
I have uttered thy spell; in the assembly of the gods I have raised thee to power,
The dominion over all the gods have I entrusted unto thee.
Be thou exalted, thou my chosen spouse,
May they magnify thy name over all of them
She hath given him the Tablets of Destiny, on his breast she laid them, saying:
'Thy command shall not be without avail, and the word of thy mouth shall be established.'
Now Kingu, thus exalted, having received the power of Anu,
Decreed the fate for the gods, her sons, saying:
'Let the opening of your mouth quench the Fire-god;
Whoso is exalted in the battle, let him display his might!"
When Ansar heard how Tiamat was mightily in revolt,
he bit his lips, his mind was not at peace,
..., he made a bitter lamentation:
... battle,
... thou...
Mummu and Apsu thou hast smitten
But Tiamat hath exalted Kingu, and where is one who can oppose her?
... deliberation
... the ... of the gods, —Nudimmud.

[A gap of about a dozen lines occurs here.]

Ansar unto his son addressed the word:
"... my mighty hero,
Whose strength is great and whose onslaught can not be withstood,
Go and stand before Tiamat,
That her spirit may be appeased, that her heart may be merciful.
But if she will not harken unto thy word,
Our word shalt thou speak unto her, that she may be pacified."
He heard the word of his father Ansar

ENUMA ELISH: THE EPIC OF CREATION

And he directed his path to her, toward her he took the way.
Ann drew nigh, he beheld the muttering of Tiamat,
But he could not withstand her, and he turned back.
... Ansar
... he spake unto him:

[A gap of over twenty lines occurs here.]

an avenger...
... valiant
... in the place of his decision
... he spake unto him:
... thy father
" Thou art my son, who maketh merciful his heart.
... to the battle shalt thou draw nigh,
he that shall behold thee shall have peace."
And the lord rejoiced at the word of his father,
And he drew nigh and stood before Ansar.
Ansar beheld him and his heart was filled with joy,
He kissed him on the lips and his fear departed from him.
"O my father, let not the word of thy lips be overcome,
Let me go, that I may accomplish all that is in thy heart.
O Ansar, let not the word of thy lips be overcome,
Let me go, that I may accomplish all that is in thy heart."
What man is it, who hath brought thee forth to battle?
... Tiamat, who is a woman, is armed and attacketh thee.
... rejoice and be glad;
The neck of Tiamat shalt thou swiftly trample under foot.
... rejoice and be glad;
The neck of Tiamat shalt thou swiftly trample under foot.
0 my son, who knoweth all wisdom,
Pacify Tiamat with thy pure incantation.
Speedily set out upon thy way,
For thy blood shall not be poured out; thou shalt return again."
The lord rejoiced at the word of his father,
His heart exulted, and unto his father he spake:

ENUMA ELISH: THE EPIC OF CREATION

"O Lord of the gods, Destiny of the great gods,
If I, your avenger,
Conquer Tiamat and give you life,
Appoint an assembly, make my fate preeminent and proclaim it.
In Upsukkinaku seat yourself joyfully together,
With my word in place of you will I decree fate.
May whatsoever I do remain unaltered,
May the word of my lips never be chanced nor made of no avail."

ENUMA ELISH: THE EPIC OF CREATION

THE THIRD TABLET

Ansar opened his mouth, and
Unto Gaga, his minister, spake the word.
"O Gaga, thou minister that rejoicest my spirit,
Unto Lahmu and Lahamu will I send thee.
... thou canst attain,
... thou shalt cause to be brought before thee.
... let the gods, all of them,
Make ready for a feast, at a banquet let them sit,
Let them eat bread, let them mix wine,
That for Marduk, their avenger they may decree the fate.
Go, Gaga, stand before them,
And all that I tell thee, repeat unto them, and say:
'Ansar, vour son, hath sent me,
The purpose of his heart he hath made known unto me.
The purpose of his heart he hath made known unto me.
He saith that Tiamat our mother hath conceived a hatred for us,
With all her force she rageth, full of wrath.
All the gods have turned to her,
With those, whom ye created, they go at her side.
They are banded together, and at the side of Tiamat they advance;
They are furious, they devise mischief without resting night and day.
They prepare for battle, fuming and raging;
They have joined their forces and are making war.
Ummu–Hubur, who formed all things,
Hath made in addition weapons invincible; she hath spawned monster–serpents,
Sharp of tooth and merciless of fang.
With poison, instead of blood, she hath filled their bodies.
Fierce monster–vipers she hath clothed with terror,
With splendor she hath decked them; she hath made them of lofty stature.
Whoever beboldeth them, terror overcometh him,
Their bodies rear up and none can withstand their attack.
She hath set up vipers, and dragons, and the monster Lahamu,

ENUMA ELISH: THE EPIC OF CREATION

And hurricanes, and raging bounds, and scorpion-men,
And mighty tempests, and fish-men, and rams;
They bear merciless weapons, without fear of the fight.
Her commands are miahty; none can. resist them;
After this fashion, huge of stature, hath she made eleven monsters.
Among the gods who are her sons, inasmuch as he hath given her support,
She hath exalted Kingu; in their midst she hath raised him to power.
To march before the forces, to lead the host,
To give the battle-signal, to advance to the attack,
To direct the battle, to control the fight,
Unto him hath she entrusted; in costly raiment she hath made him sit, saying:
I have uttered thy spell; in the assembly of the gods
I have raised thee to power,
The dominion over all the gods have I entrusted unto thee.
Be thou exalted, thou my chosen spouse,
May they magnify thy name over all of them ... the Anunnaki."
She hath given him the Tablets of Destiny, on his breast she laid them, saying:
Thy command shall not be without avail, and the word of thy mouth shall be established."
Now Kingu, thus exalted, having received the power of Anu,
Decreed the fate for the gods, her sons, saving:
Let the opening of your mouth quench the Fire-god;
Whoso is exalted in the battle, let him display his might!"
I sent Anu, but he could not withstand her;
Nudimmud was afraid and turned back.
But Marduk hath set out, the director of the gods, your son;
To set out against Tiamat his heart hath prompted him.
He opened his mouth and spake unto me, saying: "If I, your avenger,
Conquer Tiamat and give you life,
Appoint an assembly, make my fate preeminent and proclaim it.
In Upsukkinaku seat yourselves joyfully together;
With my word in place of you will I decree fate.
May whatsoever I do remain unaltered,
May the word of my lips never be changed nor made of no avail.'"
Hasten, therefore, and swiftly decree for him the fate which you bestow,
That he may go and fight your strong enemy.
Gaga went, he took his way and

ENUMA ELISH: THE EPIC OF CREATION

Humbly before Lahmu and Lahamu, the gods, his fathers,
He made obeisance, and he kissed the ground at their feet.
He humbled himself; then he stood up and spake unto them saying:
"Ansar, your son, hath sent me,
The purpose of his heart he hath made known unto me.
He saith that Tiamat our mother hath conceived a hatred for us,
With all her force she rageth, full of wrath.
All the gods have turned to her,
With those, whom ye created, they go at her side.
They are banded together and at the side of Tiamat they advance;
They are furious, they devise mischief without resting night and day.
They prepare for battle, fuming and raging;
They have joined their forces and are making war.
Ummu-Hubur, who formed all things,
Hath made in addition weapons invincible; she hath spawned monster-serpents,
Sharp of tooth and merciless of fang.
With poison, instead of blood, she hath filled their bodies.
Fierce monster-vipers she hath clothed with terror,
With splendor she hath decked them, she hath made them of lofty stature.
Whoever beboldeth them, terror overcometh him,
Their bodies rear up and none can withstand their attack.
She hath set up vipers, and dragons, and the monster Lahamu,
And hurricanes, and raging hounds, and scorpion-men,
And mighty tempests, and fish-men, and rams;
They bear merciless weapons, without fear of the fight.
Her commands are mighty; none can resist them;
After this fashion, huge of stature, hath she made eleven monsters.
Among the gods who are her sons, inasmuch as he hath given her support,
She hath exalted Kingu; in their midst she hath raised him to power.
To march before the forces, to lead the host,
To give the battle-signal, to advance to the attack, To direct the battle, to control the fight,
Unto him hath she entrusted; in costly raiment she hath made him sit, saying:
I have uttered thy spell; in the assembly of the gods I have raised thee to power,
The dominion over all the gods have I entrusted unto thee.
Be thou exalted, thou my chosen spouse,

ENUMA ELISH: THE EPIC OF CREATION

May they magnify thy name over all of them...the Anunnaki.
She hath given him the Tablets of Destiny on his breast she laid them, saving:
Thy command shall not be without avail, and the word of thy mouth shall be established.'
Now Kingu, thus exalted, having received the power of Anu,
Decreed the fate for the gods, her sons, saying:
'Let the opening of your mouth quench the Fire-god;
Whoso is exalted in the battle, let him display his might!'
I sent Anu, but he could not withstand her;
Nudimmud was afraid and turned back.
But Marduk hath set out, the director of the gods, your son;
To set out against Tiamat his heart hath prompted him.
He opened his mouth and spake unto me, saying:
'If I, your avenger,
Conquer Tiamat and give you life,
Appoint an assembly, make my fate preeminent and proclaim it.
In Upsukkinaku seat yourselves joyfully together;
With my word in place of you will I decree fate.
May, whatsoever I do remain unaltered,
May the word of my lips never be changed nor made of no avail.'
Hasten, therefore, and swiftly decree for him the fate which you bestow,
That he may go and fight your strong enemy!
Lahmu and Lahamu heard and cried aloud
All of the Igigi [The elder gods] wailed bitterly, saying:
What has been altered so that they should
We do not understand the deed of Tiamat!
Then did they collect and go,
The great gods, all of them, who decree fate.
They entered in before Ansar, they filled...
They kissed one another, in the assembly...;
They made ready for the feast, at the banquet they sat;
They ate bread, they mixed sesame-wine.
The sweet drink, the mead, confused their...
They were drunk with drinking, their bodies were filled.
They were wholly at ease, their spirit was exalted;
Then for Marduk, their avenger, did they decree the fate.

ENUMA ELISH: THE EPIC OF CREATION
THE FOURTH TABLET

They prepared for him a lordly chamber,
Before his fathers as prince he took his place.
"Thou art chiefest among the great gods,
Thy fate is unequaled, thy word is Anu!
0 Marduk, thou art chiefest among the great gods,
Thy fate is unequaled, thy word is Anu!
Henceforth not without avail shall be thy command,
In thy power shall it be to exalt and to abase.
Established shall be the word of thy mouth, irresistible shall be thy command,
None among the gods shall transgress thy boundary.
Abundance, the desire of the shrines of the gods,
Shall be established in thy sanctuary, even though they lack offerings.
O Marduk, thou art our avenger!
We give thee sovereignty over the whole world.
Sit thou down in might; be exalted in thy command.
Thy weapon shall never lose its power; it shall crush thy foe.
O Lord, spare the life of him that putteth his trust in thee,
But as for the god who began the rebellion, pour out his life."
Then set they in their midst a garment,
And unto Marduk,– their first–born they spake:
"May thy fate, O lord, be supreme among the gods,
To destroy and to create; speak thou the word, and thy command shall be fulfilled.
Command now and let the garment vanish;
And speak the word again and let the garment reappear!
Then he spake with his mouth, and the garment vanished;
Again he commanded it, and. the garment reappeared.
When the gods, his fathers, beheld the fulfillment of his word,
They rejoiced, and they did homage unto him, saying, " Marduk is king!"
They bestowed upon him the scepter, and the throne, and the ring,
They give him an invincible weapony which overwhelmeth the foe.
Go, and cut off the life of Tiamat,
And let the wind carry her blood into secret places."

ENUMA ELISH: THE EPIC OF CREATION

After the gods his fathers had decreed for the lord his fate,
They caused him to set out on a path of prosperity and success.
He made ready the bow, he chose his weapon,
He slung a spear upon him and fastened it...
He raised the club, in his right hand he grasped it,
The bow and the quiver he hung at his side.
He set the lightning in front of him,
With burning flame he filled his body.
He made a net to enclose the inward parts of Tiamat,
The four winds he stationed so that nothing of her might escape;
The South wind and the North wind and the East wind and the West wind
He brought near to the net, the gift of his father Anu.
He created the evil wind, and the tempest, and the hurricane,
And the fourfold wind, and the sevenfold wind, and the whirlwind, and the wind which had no equal;
He sent forth the winds which he bad created, the seven of them;
To disturb the inward parts of Tiamat, they followed after him.
Then the lord raised the thunderbolt, his mighty weapon,
He mounted the chariot, the storm unequaled for terror,
He harnessed and yoked unto it four horses,
Destructive, ferocious, overwhelming, and swift of pace;
... were their teeth, they were flecked with foam;
They were skilled in... , they had been trained to trample underfoot.
.... mighty in battle,
Left and right....
His garment was... , he was clothed with terror,
With overpowering brightness his head was crowned.
Then he set out, he took his way,
And toward the raging Tiamat he set his face.
On his lips he held ...,
... he grasped in his hand.
Then they beheld him, the gods beheld him,
The gods his fathers beheld him, the gods beheld him.
And the lord drew nigh, he gazed upon the inward parts of Tiamat,
He perceived the muttering of Kingu, her spouse.
As Marduk gazed, Kingu was troubled in his gait,

ENUMA ELISH: THE EPIC OF CREATION

His will was destroyed and his motions ceased.
And the gods, his helpers, who marched by his side,
Beheld their leader's..., and their sight was troubled.
But Tiamat... , she turned not her neck,
With lips that failed not she uttered rebellious words:
"... thy coming as lord of the gods,
From their places have they gathered, in thy place are they! "
Then the lord raised the thunderbolt, his mighty weapon,
And against Tiamat, who was raging, thus he sent the word:
Thou art become great, thou hast exalted thyself on high,
And thy heart hath prompted thee to call to battle.
... their fathers...,
... their... thou hatest...
Thou hast exalted Kingu to be thy spouse,
Thou hast... him, that, even as Anu, he should issue deerees.
thou hast followed after evil,
And against the gods my fathers thou hast contrived thy wicked plan.
Let then thy host be equipped, let thy weapons be girded on!
Stand! I and thou, let us join battle!
When Tiamat heard these words,
She was like one posessed, .she lost her reason.
Tiamat uttered wild, piercing cries,
She trembled and shook to her very foundations.
She recited an incantation, she pronounced her spell,
And the gods of the battle cried out for their weapons.
Then advanced Tiamat and Marduk, the counselor of the gods;
To the fight they came on, to the battle they drew nigh.
The lord spread out his net and caught her,
And the evil wind that was behind him he let loose in her face.
As Tiamat opened her mouth to its full extent,
He drove in the evil wind, while as yet she had not shut her lips.
The terrible winds filled her belly,
And her courage was taken from her, and her mouth she opened wide.
He seized the spear and burst her belly,
He severed her inward parts, he pierced her heart.
He overcame her and cut off her life;

ENUMA ELISH: THE EPIC OF CREATION

He cast down her body and stood upon it.
When be had slain Tiamat, the leader,
Her might was broken, her host was scattered.
And the gods her helpers, who marched by her side,
Trembled, and were afraid, and turned back.
They took to flight to save their lives;
But they were surrounded, so that they could not escape.
He took them captive, he broke their weapons;
In the net they were caught and in the snare they sat down.
The ... of the world they filled with cries of grief.
They received punishment from him, they were held in bondage.
And on the eleven creatures which she had filled with the power of striking terror,
Upon the troop of devils, who marched at her...,
He brought affliction, their strength he...;
Them and their opposition he trampled under his feet.
Moreover, Kingu, who had been exalted over them,
He conquered, and with the god Dug–ga he counted him.
He took from him the Tablets of Destiny that were not rightly his,
He sealed them with a seal and in his own breast he laid them.
Now after the hero Marduk had conquered and cast down his enemies,
And had made the arrogant foe even like
And had fullv established Ansar's triumph over the enemy
And had attained the purpose of Nudimmud,
Over the captive gods he strengthened his durance,
And unto Tiamat, whom be bad conquered, be returned.
And the lord stood upon Tiamat's hinder parts,
And with his merciless club he smashed her skull.
He cut through the channels of her blood,
And he made the North wind bear it away into secret places.
His fathers beheld, and they rejoiced and were glad;
Presents and gifts they brought unto him.
Then the lord rested, gazing upon her dead body,
While he divided the flesh of the ... , and devised a cunning plan.
He split her up like a flat fish into two halves;
One half of her he stablished as a covering for heaven.
He fixed a bolt, he stationed a watchman,

ENUMA ELISH: THE EPIC OF CREATION

And bade them not to let her waters come forth.
He passed through the heavens, he surveyed the regions thereof,
And over against the Deep he set the dwelling of Nudimmud.
And the lord measured the structure of the Deep,
And he founded E-sara, a mansion like unto it.
The mansion E-sara which he created as heaven,
He caused Anu, Bel, and Ea in their districts to inhabit.

ENUMA ELISH: THE EPIC OF CREATION
THE FIFTH TABLET

He (Marduk) made the stations for the great gods;
The stars, their images, as the stars of the Zodiac, he fixed.
He ordained the year and into sections he divided it;
For the twelve months he fixed three stars.
After he had ... the days of the year ... images,
He founded the station of Nibir [the planet Jupiter] to determine their bounds;
That none might err or go astray,
He set the station of Bel and Ea along with him.
He opened great gates on both sides,
He made strong the bolt on the left and on the right.
In the midst thereof he fixed the zenith;
The Moon-god he caused to shine forth, the night he entrusted to him.
He appointed him, a being of the night, to determine the days;
Every month without ceasing with the crown he covered him, saying:
"At the beginning of the month, when thou shinest upon the land,
Thou commandest the horns to determine six days,
And on the seventh day to divide the crown.
On the fourteenth day thou shalt stand opposite, the half....
When the Sun-god on the foundation of heaven...thee,
The ... thou shalt cause to ..., and thou shalt make his...
... unto the path of the Sun-god shalt thou cause to draw nigh,
And on the ... day thou shalt stand opposite, and the Sun-god shall...
... to traverse her way.
... thou shalt cause to draw nigh, and thou shalt judge the right.
... to destroy..."

[Nearly fifty lines are here lost.]

The gods, his fathers, beheld the net which he had made,
They beheld the bow and how its work was accomplished.
They praised the work which he had done...
Then Anu raised the ... in the assembly of the gods. He kissed the bow, saving, " It is...!"

ENUMA ELISH: THE EPIC OF CREATION

And thus he named the names of the bow, saying,
"'Long-wood' shall be one name, and the second name shall be ...,
And its third name shall be the Bow-star, in heaven shall it...!"
Then he fixed a station for it...
Now after the fate of...
He set a throne...
...in heaven...
[The remainder of this tablet is missing.]

ENUMA ELISH: THE EPIC OF CREATION
THE SIXTH TABLET

When Marduk beard the word of the gods,
His heart prompted him and he devised a cunning plan.
He opened his mouth and unto Ea he spake
That which he had conceived in his heart he imparted unto him:
"My blood will I take and bone will I fashion
I will make man, that man may
I will create man who shall inhabit the earth,
That the service of the gods may be established, and that their shrines may be built.
But I will alter the ways of the gods, and I will change their paths;
Together shall they be oppressed and unto evil shall they....
And Ea answered him and spake the word:
"... the ... of the gods I have changed
... and one...
... shall be destroyed and men will I...
... and the gods .
... and they..."

[The rest of the text is wanting with the exception of
the last few lines of the tablet, which read as follows.]

They rejoiced...
In Upsukkinnaku they set their dwelling.
Of the heroic son, their avenger, they cried:
" We, whom he succored.... !"

They seated themselves and in the assembly they named him...,
They all cried aloud, they exalted him...

ENUMA ELISH: THE EPIC OF CREATION

THE SEVENTH TABLET

O Asari, [Marduk] "Bestower of planting," "Founder of sowing"
"Creator of grain and plants," "who caused the green herb to spring up!"
O Asaru–alim, [Mardk] "who is revered in the house of counsel," "who aboundeth in counsel,"
The gods paid homage, fear took hold upon them!

O Asaru–alim–nuna, [Marduk] "the mighty one," "the Light of the father who begat him,"
"Who directeth the decrees of Anu Bel, and Ea!"
He was their patron, be ordained their...;
He, whose provision is abundance, goeth forth...
Tutu [Marduk] is "He who created them anew";
Should their wants be pure, then are they satisfied;
Should he make an incantation, then are the gods appeased;
Should they attack him in anger, he withstandeth their onslaught!
Let him therefore be exalted, and in the assembly of the gods let him... ;
None among the gods can rival him!
15 Tutu [Marduk] is Zi–ukkina, "the Life of the host of the gods,"
Who established for the gods the bright heavens.
He set them on their way, and ordained their path;
Never shall his ... deeds be forgotten among men.
Tutu as Zi–azag thirdly they named, "the Bringer of Purification,"
"The God of the Favoring Breeze," "the Lord of Hearing and Mercy,"
"The Creator of Fulness and Abundance," " the Founder of Plenteousness,"
"Who increaseth all that is small."
In sore distress we felt his favoring breeze,"
Let them say, let them pay reverence, let them bow in humility before him!
Tutu as Aga–azag may mankind fourthly magnify!
"The Lord of the Pure Incantation," " the Quickener of the Dead,"
"Who had mercy upon the captive gods,"
"Who removed the yoke from upon the gods his enemies,"
"For their forgiveness did he create mankind,"

ENUMA ELISH: THE EPIC OF CREATION

"The Merciful One, with whom it is to bestow life!"
May his deeds endure, may they never be forgotten ,
In the mouth of mankind whom his hands have made!
Tutu as Mu-azag, fifthly, his "Pure incantation" may their mouth proclaim,
Who through his Pure Incantation hath destroyed all the evil ones!"
Sag-zu, [Marduk] "who knoweth the heart of the gods," " who seeth through the innermost part!"
"The evil-doer he hath not caused to go forth with him!"
"Founder of the assembly of the gods," who ... their heart!"
"Subduer of the disobedient," "...!"
"Director of Righteousness," "...,"
" Who rebellion and...!"
Tutu as Zi-si, "the ...,"
"Who put an end to anger," "who...!"
Tutu as Suh-kur, thirdly, "the Destroyer of the foe,"
"Who put their plans to confusion,"
"Who destroyed all the wicked," "...,"
... let them... !

[There is a gap here of sixty lines. But somewhere among the lost lines belong the following fragments.]

who...
He named the four quarters of the world, mankind hecreated,
And upon him understanding...
"The mighty one...!"
Agil...
"The Creator of the earth...!"
Zulummu... .
"The Giver of counsel and of whatsoever...!"
Mummu, " the Creator of...!"
Mulil, the heavens...,
"Who for...!"
Giskul, let...,
"Who brought the gods to naught....!"
....

ENUMA ELISH: THE EPIC OF CREATION

... " the Chief of all lords,"
... supreme is his might!
Lugal–durmah, "the King of the band of the gods," " the Lord of rulers."
"Who is exalted in a royal habitation,"
"Who among the gods is gloriously supreme!
Adu–nuna, " the Counselor of Ea," who created the gods his fathers,
Unto the path of whose majesty
No god can ever attain!
... in Dul–azag be made it known,
... pure is his dwelling!
... the... of those without understanding is Lugaldul–azaga!
... supreme is his might!
... their... in the midst of Tiamat,
... of the battle!

[Here follows the better–preserved ending.]

... the star, which shineth in the heavens.
May he hold the Beginning and the Future, may they pay homage unto him,
Saying, "He who forced his way through the midst of Tiamat without resting,
Let his name be Nibiru, 'the Seizer of the Midst'!
For the stars of heaven he upheld the paths,
He shepherded all the gods like sheep!
He conquered Tiamat, he troubled and ended her life,"
In the future of mankind, when the days grow old,
May this be heard without ceasing; may it hold sway forever!
Since he created the realm of heaven and fashioned the firm earth,
The Lord of the World," the father Bel hath called his name.
This title, which all the Spirits of Heaven proclaimed,
Did Ea hear, and his spirit was rejoiced, and he said:
"He whose name his fathers have made glorious,
Shall be even as I, his name shall be Ea!
The binding of all my decrees shall he control,
All my commands shall he make known! "
By the name of "Fifty " did the great gods
Proclaim his fifty names, they, made his path preeminent.

ENUMA ELISH: THE EPIC OF CREATION

EPILOGUE

Let them [i.e. the names of Marduk] be held in remembrances and let the first man proclaim them;
Let the wise and the understanding consider them together!
Let the father repeat them and teach them to his son;
Let them be in the ears of the pastor and the shepherd!
Let a man rejoice in Marduk, the Lord of the gods,
That be may cause his land to be fruitful, and that he himself may have prosperity!
His word standeth fast, his command is unaltered;
The utterance of his mouth hath no god ever annulled.
He gazed in his anger, he turned not his neck;
When he is wroth, no god can withstand his indignation.
Wide is his heart, broad is his compassion;
The sinner and evil-doer in his presence...
They received instruction, they spake before him,
... unto...
... of Marduk may the gods...;
... May they ... his name... !
... they took and...
................................!

END OF THE CREATION EPIC
THE FIGHT WITH TIAMAT

(ANOTHER VERSION)
[Note: Strictly speaking, the text is not a creation-legend, though it gives a variant form of the principal incident in the history of the creation according to the Enuma Elish. Here the fight with the dragon did not precede the creation of the world, but took place after men had been created and cities had been built.]

The cities sighed, men ...
Men uttered lamentation, they ...
For their lamentation there was none to help,
For their grief there was none to take them by the hand.

ENUMA ELISH: THE EPIC OF CREATION

á Who was the dragon... ?
Tiamat was the dragon.....
Bel in heaven hath formed.....
Fifty kaspu [A kaspu is the space that can be covered in two hours travel, i.e. six or seven miles] in his length, one kaspu in his height,
Six cubits is his mouth, twelve cubits his...,
Twelve cubits is the circuit of his ears...;
For the space of sixty cubits he ... a bird;
In water nine cubits deep he draggeth...."
He raiseth his tail on high...;
All the gods of heaven...
In heaven the gods bowed themselves down before the Moon-god...;
The border of the Moon-god's robe they hastily grasped:
"Who will go and slay the dragon,"
And deliver the broad land from...
And become king over... ?
" Go, Tishu, slav the dragon,
And deliver the broad land from...,
And become king over...!"
Thou hast sent me, O Lord, to... the raging creatures of the river,
But I know not the... of the Dragon!

[The rest of the Obverse and the upper part of the Reverse of the tablet are wanting.]

REVERSE
....
And opened his mouth and spake unto the god...
" Stir up cloud, and storm and tempest!
The seal of thy life shalt thou set before thy face,
Thou shalt grasp it, and thou shalt slay the dragon."
He stirred up cloud, and storm and tempest,
He set the seal of his life before his face,
He grasped it, and he slew the dragon.
For three years and three months, one day and one night
The blood of the dragon flowed. ...

CPSIA information can be obtained at www.ICGtesting.com
Printed in the USA
BVOW06s1111031113
335346BV00004B/38/P